D0559137

The Legend

The Mystery of Herobrine, Book One - The Start of a Quest (The Unofficial Minecraft Adventure Story)

Mark Mulle

PUBLISHED BY:
Mark Mulle
Copyright © 2014

There were two of us in the beginning: my friend, Jerry, and me. My name is Mike, by the way. We spawned in this forest biome, on top of a big mountain. The mountain was so high that snow tiles covered the top of it. We could see far away, across a giant sea of dark green trees.

My friend, Jerry, knew a lot more about Minecraft than I did, so naturally, I followed his lead in everything.

It was the middle of the day, from what I gathered. The giant yellow square that was the sun was right above us.

"We should get to the bottom of the Mountain and start gathering some resources. We'll probably make it safely down before the sun goes down and monsters start crawling around the place," said Jerry.

"You're right. But don't get too far ahead," I told him.

"Don't worry, I won't. Just try to stay close to me. Don't go jumping down without looking ahead first. We don't have any food yet, so try not getting hurt. Okay?"

"Sure thing, Jerry," I told him.

"Right, let's go!"

Jerry turned around and started climbing down the mountain, jumping down one square at a time. I followed him closely.

As we were climbing down we began to see sheep. They were in small groups of three to five sheep, huddled together. As we walked past them they turned their small, square-shaped heads and looked at us. Jerry went close to one and started punching it. I quickly did the same and started bashing the sheep that was closest to me. As I hit the sheep, it started turning red with each hit. I know what you're thinking, but sheep are a valuable resource in Minecraft. They provide both meat and wool, two important resources that a player needs in order to survive. So, in a matter of minutes, the two sheep each turned into meat and two squares of white wool. The other sheep ran away, scattering in every direction. Jerry and I gathered the items that the sheep dropped.

"We best let the others go. Let's focus on getting to the bottom of this mountain and harvesting some other resources," said Jerry.

"You're the pro," I told him.

And so we kept going down the mountain. Jerry was getting pretty far ahead from me, running and jumping. I noticed that when you run and jump at a certain angle, not only can you jump further but you can also reduce the damage that you take when falling. But don't get carried away, though, I'm talking about a distance of a few blocks that are not at a big angle.

We got to the bottom of the mountain just in time. As the sun went down, the sky turned different shades of red and purple.

Jerry walked up to a tall tree, an oak I think. It must have been ten or fifteen blocks high. Jerry started punching the base of it with his bare hands. The wooden block started splintering into small brown particles. After a few seconds we heard a popping sound and the tree block disappeared and reappeared as a smaller block, spinning on the ground. Jerry turned to me after picking the small block.

"Look. You smash the tree and get the block. You then pick it up from your inventory and turn it into wooden planks."

"Okay, I'll give it a go," I told him.

I did exactly as I saw him do it. It seemed that it took forever to destroy the wooden block.

"Don't worry, Mike. Chopping down trees will get much easier once we craft the proper tools, you'll see," Jerry assured me.

Finally, I managed to chop down the tree. Gosh, it took quite some time. I collected the block and turned it into some wooden planks.

"What now?" I asked Jerry.

"Well, now we use four planks in order to create a Crafting Table," said Jerry.

I did just that.

"Now take the Crafting Table, and set it right here on the ground," said Jerry.

"Okay."

I created the Crafting Table and put it right next to the tree that I just started chopping.

"Cool, just like that. Now let's gather another block of wood. I'll show you how to craft an axe," said Jerry.

Again, I started punching away at the oak trunk. I finally managed to chop down yet another block of oak wood with my bare hands and I walked up to Jerry. His tree was already gone. The leaves from the tree still hovered around the space that was once occupied by the tree itself. Jerry had a wooden axe in his hand.

"How did...you..." I mumbled.

"What? The axe? Come on, I'll teach you how to do it. It's so simple, you'll see. Walk up to your Crafting Table and craft some wooden planks. That's right. Now use two planks, one on top of each other and craft some sticks. That's it. Now use two sticks and the rest of your wooden planks and this extra one. Here! Use your imagination. The sticks form the handle and you make the blade out of three wooden planks. It will make sense after you see it, trust me."

I followed his instructions and on the third go at arranging the planks, I managed to craft myself my first Minecraft tool – a trusty wooden axe.

"There you go," said Jerry. "Now get to chopping some more wood. You can never have enough wood. Trust me. I'll tell you when to stop. We still have a lot of crafting to do."

So I equipped my wooden axe and started chopping down trees left and right.

The night came quickly and after what seemed as few minutes, darkness fell over the forest. We could hear the groaning of zombies. Jerry came over to where I was working on chopping a small tree.

"Come on! Follow me", said Jerry. "First, use your axe and chop down your Crafting Table, collect it and let's get out of here. Quickly!"

I ran over to my crafting table and in a matter of seconds my Crafting Table was inside my inventory.

"I'm ready. Let's go," I told Jerry.

"Good. I think the zombies might be closing in on us," said Jerry.

The both of us ran to the side of the mountain that we had climbed down from and Jerry took out his wooden pickaxe. He then started using it to dig into the mountain. Within minutes he had dug a tunnel that was just two blocks high, enough for us to go inside. He suddenly turned around.

"Here! Take this. Two diggers are faster than one," he said.

"Let's do this!"

So I picked up the pickaxe and started expanding the tunnel into a small room. I even managed to find a block or two of coal and so did Jerry.

"Okay, that should do it," said Jerry as he set his Crafting Table next to a wall.

He then used the table and crafted some torches. He then set two torches on opposite walls.

"Torches, Mike. Never leave home without them. Remember that," he said.

"I'll make sure to remember it," I told him.

"Good. Now you craft a wooden door, okay? It's the simplest thing: just six wooden planks, two columns, three blocks high and put it over there, so the monsters don't come in," said Jerry.

I followed his instructions and crafted the wooden door. I then walked up to the entrance of our small shelter and placed it on the ground and presto! We now had a wooden door to keep us safe from the monsters that roamed the forest at night.

As I turned around, I saw that Jerry had already constructed a furnace.

"We will use the furnace to cook our food, but we can do loads of other things with it, though. We can melt iron blocks into ingots with it, we can melt gold…Remember that, too. As a matter of fact, remember these things: Crafting Table, axe and pickaxe, furnace and torches," said Jerry.

"Got it!"

As the night went on, Jerry showed me how to craft a lot of things including torches, swords, shovels and he even taught me how to craft a bed, although we didn't have enough wool to do that, unfortunately. By the way, a bed is kind of an important thing in Minecraft. Not only can you sleep in it, in order to make the night go by faster, but you can also respawn there after dying; well you actually spawn next to it, not in it. Also, if you happen to get your hands on a compass, it will always lead you back to your bed.

Even without a bed, the night went by quite fast, as I was trying to soak up as much information as I could from Jerry.

Finally, when the sun came up, the both of us went out into the forest once more.

"We need to gather some more materials," said Jerry. "You focus on harvesting some more wood and I'll try to find some animals. Maybe I'll find some more sheep so we can have some more food. Keep a look out. There may be other players. This place is quite old, but I don't think it's deserted."

"Ok. I'll be sure to have my sword close by," I told him.

And just like that, Jerry disappeared, climbing his way back onto the mountain. I, however, made sure that I didn't get too far away from our camp.

By the time Jerry got back in the afternoon I managed to clear up quite a lot of the trees in the immediate vicinity of our camp. I had gathered about a stack of oak wood and a few apples, too. I also gathered some seeds.

Jerry managed to come back with quite a lot of meat and wool. He then proceeded to cook the meat and craft a couple of beds for us to sleep in.

Two days had passed from the time that we had spawned on top of the mountain and our little cave began to look much more like a home.

"Don't get too used to it, though," Jerry told me. "We'll gather as many and as much as we can carry and then we will set off to find a more hospitable place. But first thing's first: we'll start digging a mine tomorrow and we'll start looking for some iron."

A mine! I couldn't wait to start digging deep into the earth. I heard that you could find all sorts of interesting things when digging deep enough. From resources like gold and iron, to things like lapis lazuli, which is a blue rock of some sorts, or red stone that you can use to build all sorts of contraptions.

And so, on the next day we started digging our way into the depths of the earth. The digging went pretty fast, I must say. At least I think it did. You kind of lose the track of time while you're digging, because you don't see the sun rising or setting.

We kept digging for hours on end and we found all sorts of stuff. We also kept close to one another, as it's pretty easy to get lost when you're digging.

I managed to find a large number of coal blocks, all bunched together. I started smashing the blocks with my pickaxe. The blocks cracked and turned into small pieces of coal that flew left and right. And as I laid waste to a coal block, I discovered another under it. I kept smashing away. Almost all of them were gone and the coal went into my inventory. I was quite proud of myself for harvesting so much coal. As I looked around, I saw that there was but one coal block left – the one that was under me. I started picking away at it. Jerry turned around and saw what I was doing. The coal block was splintering and at that moment I heard Jerry.

"Don't dig straight down, Mike!"

But it was too late. I had already managed to destroy the block of coal from under me. Coal started flying everywhere and I fell. I kept falling and falling until I hit water.

I managed to swim to the surface and looked around. The light was very dim, but I could see a source of red light in the distance. I could hear Jerry's voice from above.

"I thought I told you to NEVER dig straight down! Come on!"

"Sorry, Jerry! I'm fine, though. I managed to land straight in the water," I yelled.

"Just stay put! I'm going to jump in there and help you come back up. Maybe we'll find some stuff down there. Just stay put, okay?"

"Okay"

Jerry then jumped through the hole and landed right next to me in the underground river.

"Okay, let's get to the shore. Keep your sword close. It's pretty dark in here so we might run into monsters," said Jerry.

And he was right, as soon as we got on dry land zombies started swarming towards us. We managed to fight our way through them and got into a small crack in the giant cavern wall. The crack was small enough for us to fight the zombies one by one. The zombies were relentless. About ten, green-skinned, lumbering, non-dead creatures tried their best to kill us. They quickly blocked the entrance to our newly-found shelter and launched attack after attack. Jerry and I stood shoulder to shoulder and lunged our stone swords at the monsters. We managed to land blow after blow, and with each hit the zombies turned red and bounced back. But with each zombie that we managed to turn away, two more would take its place. I got hit a couple of times, but luckily, it wasn't enough to knock me down or separate me from my friend. In about five minutes, we managed to kill all the zombies. But as we got out of the crack within the wall, we heard a hissing noise. Quickly, the noise got louder and louder and then there was an explosion.

Apparently, while we were busy fighting off the zombies, a creeper managed to make his way right next to us. The explosion scattered a bunch of stone blocks from the cavern wall and it took a sizeable chunk out of our health bars. Jerry was the closest to the explosion, so he received most of the damage.

"Are you okay?"

"I'm fine. But we best eat something and get out of here and we better do it fast," said Jerry.

We both got out some cooked meat and ate it as we got closer and closer to the light source in the distance.

The light source turned out to be a great lava river that cascaded from the side of the crevasse and split into multiple rivers when it hit the cave floor. The rivers then flowed directly into the water. The light from all that lava lit the entire wall and most of the cave. We could see iron blocks, gold blocks and even some lapis lazuli.

"Well, we'd better make the most of our journey into this dark place. Stay close," said Jerry.

We then managed to build ourselves a small shelter into the cave wall and we crafted about six furnaces to help us melt whatever material we found into ingots.

I don't exactly know how much time we spent there, but we did manage to find a lot of materials. We crafted ourselves a couple of full armor sets out of iron: helmet, breastplate, greaves and boots. We also crafted a nice set of iron tools. Stone tools are ok, but iron tools are much better.

After I crafted my armor and my tools, I became more and more confident. I started wandering further and further away from Jerry and went on searches for materials all by myself. I managed not to get lost, because I had a system: whenever I wandered off by myself, I o built these small pillars that indicated the way back. Clever, right?

We managed to gather stacks upon stacks of resources and we decided to give the small tunnels that riddled the cave wall a try. That was a good thing as we managed to find even more iron and gold.

As I was digging away at an iron vein I heard this strange noise coming from the ground. It was deep and pretty scary. Jerry heard it too.

"What is that?" I asked Jerry.

"It's probably a mineshaft," he said.

"What's a mineshaft?"

"It's exactly what it sounds like. It's an abandoned mineshaft. It looks really cool and you can find all sorts of cool stuff in it. Imagine all the mine tunnels that we dug so far, but only cooler."

"So, are we going to look for it, or what," I anxiously asked him.

"Not today we won't. We're running low on food. We should focus on getting back to the surface and finding some more food. We still have some meat inside that chest of ours, but we will probably have to find more food. Maybe even build ourselves a small farm and plant some crops."

After a couple of minutes we managed to harvest all the raw materials that were inside that tunnel. We then reached the main cave and headed to our shelter, in order to get the materials that we had put inside the furnaces.

We walked inside the shelter and emptied all the furnaces. But when we turned around and headed for the exit, we saw a long pair of black legs.

"Enderman," said Jerry. "We'd best be careful. These guys are tough and we don't know exactly how many of them are out there. There could be just this guy or there could be more of them waiting for us."

"How do we get past him?"

"We need some water. Water hurts these guys. We grab a bucket full and dump it near him. When the water touches him, he gets hurt and teleports himself away from it," he explained.

"Well do we have any water? I don't," I told him.

"Me neither," he said.

"We could always dig past him. Couldn't we? I mean we can dig through the side wall and keep digging and turn right and reach the main cave," I told him.

"We could do that, I guess. We don't even need to get that far away from him," said Jerry.

"What do you mean? Won't he see us?" I asked.

"He will. But Endermen are different from other monsters. They see you, but they won't attack you, unless you attack them first or unless you look them straight in the eye. For some reason, they really do not like that," he said. "I will start digging past him. Follow my lead, and whatever you do, don't hit him and don't, I repeat, do not look him in the eye, or we are both toast."

"Understood. Lead the way," I told him.

Jerry started digging carefully, block after block. After two sets of blocks were destroyed, he started making his way out. He managed to destroy another three sets of blocks and finally we reached the main cave. I looked right and saw the tall, dark shape of the Enderman. He had long legs and long thin arms. His whole body was black except for his eyes. His eyes were big and white, with two small spots of pink or purple – it was too dark for me to tell. The dark creature had a stone block in his hands. He turned around and looked at us. I kept repeating in my mind: *don't look him in the eyes, don't look him in the eyes, don't look him in the eyes*.

Jerry whispered:

"Come on, let's go. Stop looking at him; you'll probably end up looking him straight in the eye, just like I did the first time I was in Minecraft. Come on, move your feet."

I turned around and followed Jerry. We walked along the banks of the underground river in which I initially fell. We walked at a moderate pace. Running in the dark will only get you in dangerous places. And from time to time we would drop a torch in order to keep the way lit up for when we would return in search for other useful raw materials or even to explore that abandoned mineshaft that Jerry was talking about. We walked for quite some time until Jerry and I recognized the place where we took cover when the zombies swarmed us and where we almost got blown to bits by that ghastly creeper. Small blocks of stone were still hovering near that area. We placed several torches on the walls and on the floor to make sure that no monsters would spawn out of the darkness and ambush us out of the blue.

We figured that the hole through which I fell into the river and inside this giant ravine wasn't far. The torches that we set managed to light up the cave pretty

well, but not enough for us to spot a tiny
hole in the roof.

"We should start building a stairv
close to the roof. We stand a better chan~~ ~~ ~~~~ ~
the exit when we will be nearer to the roof than if we
look for it from down here," said Jerry.

I knew that we had a lot of stone blocks in our
inventories so building a thin stairway wouldn't have
taken us that much time to build. And in fact, it didn't.
Within a few minutes we found ourselves halfway to
the roof. The stairway that we had built so far was
pretty tall, but it only reached half the distance. It was a
very thin structure and I bet that from afar it looked
pretty funny. Luckily, the laws of physics don't fully
apply in Minecraft, or we would have been falling pretty
fast into the river and all that stone would have sunk to
the bottom of it.

"There it is, Jerry!"

"Where?"

"Right there!"

I started building again, laying block after block
of stone and gradually making my way up to the hole in
the roof. In a few minutes we were through the hole
and into our initial mine tunnel and a few minutes after
that we were back inside our original shelter.

I felt pretty good about finally being home,
even if home meant a smaller cave dug into the side of
a mountain. We deposited all the materials that we had
mined inside a couple of big wooden chests next to our
beds. We then ate some of the food that we had left
over and headed outside.

It was the middle of the day, so Jerry went out
hunting again and I focused on trying to acquire some
more seeds in order to plant some nice wheat crops.

By the time the day was over, Jerry came back with quite a hefty quantity of provisions of meat and some leather, too. Apparently, he managed to find some cows. I, however, managed to build a small farm that could give us enough wheat for us to bake a sizeable amount of bread.

"So did you scout the area?" I asked Jerry.

"I did, but so far I didn't find much, apart from trees and hills. Not many animals, either. A few cows, but no pigs or cats or dogs, not even more sheep. The forest looks pretty empty," he said.

"Well that's not good," I concluded.

"No it is not. We should bunch up our resources and head back down the tunnels tomorrow and see what we find in that abandoned mineshaft. We can empty that whole area and then draw out a plan to move camp somewhere else," said Jerry.

"Sounds good to me," I told him.

And so we cooked the food and repaired our tools, because they were pretty much near breaking point from all the wear-and-tear that came with all that fighting and mining from the day before.

When the night came we got a good night's sleep and in the morning we packed our inventories full of provisions and headed down the tunnel.

We carefully descended into the earth's depths once more. As we went down we could hear the growls of zombies at every corner and the crackling of bones and winding of bows. It seemed like we were gone, monsters crawled out of the dark corners and started spreading out through our tunnels.

It didn't take long until we were face to face with a small pack of zombies that was accompanied by three skeletons.

The zombies charged right at us. I huddled up with my back to the wall, thinking that in doing so, I wouldn't be caught from behind. Two zombies attacked me, arms flailing. I used my iron sword and started smashing away at their heads. The first zombie was easy to dispatch of, but the second zombie charged rapidly after his companion disappeared in a puff of smoke. I managed to duck out of the way as he rushed towards me. But then out of the blue something hit me. One of the skeletons fired an arrow at me and managed to hit me dead on. The arrow hit my armor with a loud bang and managed not only to chip away at my health bar, but also to send me back a couple of feet and interrupt my attack on the zombie. Seeing that I was thrown off my guard, the zombie that was attacking me rushed with even more rage. At that point, I turned my back and ran around the corner. I then stopped and turned around, awaiting my attacker. The unsuspecting zombie followed me through the tunnel and when he turned the corner after me, I started wailing on him with my sword. I managed to land every blow, and with each successful hit, the zombie went back a few paces. Finally, I managed to destroy him for good.

Realizing that I had left my friend behind, I quickly turned around and ran towards the battle scene that I had previously abandoned. When I arrived, I saw that Jerry was overwhelmed by the monsters. He kept pushing them away with his sword and trying to dodge the incoming arrows that the skeletons were firing at him.

I rushed to my friend's side and managed to kill a zombie within the first seconds from entering the battle.

Both of us killed the remaining zombies quite easily, but there remained the skeletons. They were a tricky bunch, as they were at quite a distance, meaning that we would have a hard time reaching them without getting riddled with arrows. I, like the noob I was, charged the skeletons full on. This was not a wise idea, because it meant that they could fire their arrows at me pretty easily and hit me almost every time. Luckily I had a stack of cobblestone handy. I switched my sword with the cobblestone stack and built myself a two-block pillar behind which I could hide, in order to heal myself from the wounds that the arrows had inflicted upon me. From behind the pillar I could see Jerry reaching the skeletons. Having a lot more experience than me, Jerry knew that in order to successfully defeat skeletons, you had to run up to them in a zigzag pattern and not charge them head-on. He ran diagonally from one wall to the other and when he finally reached them, he positioned himself in front of one of the skeletons in such a manner that the other could not hit him with his arrows unless he fired at his own friend. Pretty smart, don't you think? This way Jerry managed to destroy one of the skeletons using not only his own iron sword, but also benefiting from the "help" of the other skeleton. You see, skeletons are not that smart, so the second skeleton kept aiming for Jerry. Jerry kept using the first skeleton as cover, thus, the second skeleton had to fire at his own friend. Within seconds, the first skeleton had perished by Jerry's iron sword and by his own friend's arrows. Jerry then attacked the second skeleton. Jerry furiously swept his sword at the remaining skeleton. Each time he brought the sword down on the monster, the monster would flash red and jump a couple of feet back. But getting hurt didn't stop the monster from firing more arrows at Jerry. Finally, my friend managed to push the monster up against a wall and smashed him completely with his sword.

I came out from behind my cover feeling a bit ashamed that I did not help my friend defeat the skeletons.

"Are you alright, Jerry?"

"I'm fine. But those monsters aren't. We didn't even make it to the bottom of the tunnel this time. Where do all these monsters come from?"

"I have no idea," I confessed to Jerry.

"There must be some other portions of tunnels where we forgot to put torches in. Never mind, let's get down there and check out that abandoned mineshaft."

And so we continued our journey into the dark recesses of the earth.

After about ten minutes, we found ourselves climbing down the stone stairway that we had constructed not too long ago. We didn't run, though, as the steps were pretty narrow and the way down was pretty steep. We didn't really realize how hazardous was the stairway when building it up. In fact, it seemed fine when we were building it, but we couldn't say the same thing right now, when we were going the other way.

Eventually, we managed to navigate safely down the stairway and reach the lava river. Jerry led the way. He suddenly stopped.

"I'm pretty sure that we didn't lay down that many torches," he said in a concerned tone.

"I think we did", I told him. "Who else would lay down these torches? We haven't seen anyone the past few days."

"Still…Keep your sword drawn, just to be sure we don't get caught off guard. Sometimes people can be worse than monsters in Minecraft," said Jerry.

That last thing that he said had me feeling a bit worried. What did he mean by "People can be worse than monsters in Minecraft"? I mean, why would anyone act that way?

We cautiously made our way down the tunnel in which we suspected the mineshaft would be and we started hearing that noise again. The strange noise seemed to be coming from underneath our feet. I took out my pickaxe and starting digging, but not straight down, this time. Fool me once! After digging through about four layers of stone floor, I managed to find a block of wood. I turned around and saw that Jerry wasn't there anymore. I figured that he had wandered off for a bit and that I should continue my excavation. I took out my iron axe and hacked the wooden block away. The brown block revealed a small tunnel, weakly lit by a torch from somewhere. I jumped down the small hole, as the distance didn't seem all that big. I landed in a fraction of a second in what seemed like a narrow tunnel carved into the stone. The tunnel had beams of wood once every five blocks or so that had the role to support the ceiling and keep the tunnel from collapsing from its own weight. Not particularly useful, I guess, since again, Minecraft does not care that much for the laws of physics, but the wooden beams added a lot to the atmosphere of the whole thing. I felt like a true adventurer. I slowly walked around the tunnel and saw that there even were some wooden tracks laid out on the floor and a small mine cart with a wooden container in it. I opened the container and found three loafs of bread, an iron pickaxe, a couple of gold ingots and an emerald. The green crystal seemed to radiate this beautiful green color in the darkness of the mineshaft. I didn't actually know its purpose or in fact how to use it, but I figured it looked pretty cool, not to mention valuable, so I kept it. After I stored the emerald in my inventory, I then destroyed and collected the mine cart, along with the chest that was inside it and the wooden rails that were beneath it. For a moment there, I thought about the idea of Jerry and me building our own rail track leading into the depths of the earth, just like in those fantasy stories about dwarves and goblins. We would have our own mine from which we would siphon all sorts of riches and live like kings.

My fantasy was then abruptly interrupted by a large number of red eyes that gazed at me from within a dark corner of the tunnel and by some worrisome hissing noises.

"What the..." but I never got to finish my question, because in a matter of seconds I was already swarmed by a large number of spiders. There were both black and green, eight-legged, red-eyed monstrosities chasing me down the tunnels. I ran for my life. The only thing that I could think of was *Where is Jerry? How did I manage to get lost from him?* I ran through the winding tunnels until I found myself within a poorly lit, narrow corridor. I managed to see something in the distance. It looked white. Maybe it was some sort of light source or...

By the time I had reached the object in the distance I felt a knot in my stomach. The white object to which I was heading was in fact a spider web. Not only was the narrow corridor filled with it, but all the spiders had chased behind me and I was now caught right in the middle of the whole thing. Going forward through the spider web was severely slow and in a couple of seconds the spiders had caught up to me. I turned around, facing the spiders, and slashed at the nearest one – a big green spider with hideous red eyes. I managed to land a couple of blows right on the spider's ugly head, but shortly after the last blow, the spider bit me. My skin flashed red and my health bar turned green and rapidly started decreasing. I was poisoned. My impending death, eaten by spiders in some abandoned mineshaft, down in the middle of the earth, became the only thing that I could think about. I mean, sure, I could respawn, but I would lose all of my XP points and all of my items along with my precious emerald. And where was Jerry? Those thoughts turned quickly into rage as I decided that instead of defending myself and waiting for the spiders or the poison to defeat me, I would turn the tables on them and launch into a desperate attack. I then started moving forward hacking and slashing away at everything that had more than two legs. Two black spiders fell rather quickly followed by another two green spiders and it seemed like my attackers' numbers were quickly dwindling. I destroyed yet another pair of spiders and found myself thinking that that was it. That is, until I heard the hissing of four more spiders, this time, coming from behind me. I took a quick glance at my health bar and saw that I had enough health to endure one more blow. I then quickly turned around and ran for my life yet again, but this time I ran down the corridor on the same path that I had used to get there. Of course, the spiders followed me closely, but not close enough so that they could touch me.

As I took a right turn down the next tunnel I noticed that the light was much brighter. I then heard a familiar voice.

"In here!"

I looked around and saw Jerry standing inside a small hole in the wall. I ran up to him and entered the small shelter. We traded places inside and Jerry positioned himself between me and my eight-legged attackers. He then started wailing on them with his iron sword. He destroyed the four spiders within seconds. He had a neat strategy though: instead of focusing on one spider, he used his sword to knock back one spider at a time so that none of them could surprise him and poison him while he was busy with just one spider. He managed to destroy all of them in quite a short time.

After the spiders were all destroyed, we healed up and started wondering the abandoned mineshaft together.

"Where did you go?" I asked Jerry. "I almost got killed out there."

"Sorry, I guess I just wandered off. I thought I saw something lurking in the shadows and I went off to investigate. I should have told you."

"It's okay. I'm alright now. Thanks for saving my behind, yet again. I guess I should have stopped digging and wait for you to come back."

"Did you find anything?"

"Oh yes," I told him, barely containing my enthusiasm. "I found this mine cart with a container in it, a wooden chest in which I found some bread, some gold and...an emerald. Isn't that cool?"

"It is," said Jerry.

"What can I do with it? The emerald I mean," I asked him.

"Well, you can use it to trade with villagers. That is, if we find any villagers," he responded.

I was pretty disappointed by that. At least the emerald looked kind of cool.

After we were completely healed we started making our way together through the tunnels. We collected all sorts of useful stuff: iron, gold, more provisions and even some healing potions found in one of the mine carts.

As we walked down one of the tunnels we found a stairway that wound its way down a deep tunnel.

I went down the stairs and saw a red glow coming from the end of the tunnel. When we reached the end of the tunnel we saw a small pool of lava that spread a reddish glow to the entire portion of the cave.

"Well this looks strange," pointed Jerry.

One portion of the room had a very large hole that gaped itself into the wall. The hole was dark and had rail tracks coming out of it, but no mine cart on them. The hole was very irregular, with blocks missing sporadically.

A small stream of lava came out of the wall near the hole and flowed down the floor into the pool. As I walked around I could see that there were small holes, the size of two or three blocks carved into the stone wall around the pool, with stone blocks in the lava, leading up to them like some sort of walkway.

Jerry found a wooden chest and quickly investigated.

"There's nothing in here except for this iron pickaxe," he said.

I nodded and walked up to the giant hole in the wall.

"This looks like a tunnel to me. Do you think somebody made this?"

"Quite possibly," said Jerry.

"Do you think that we should investigate?"

"I don't know," confessed Jerry.

But without thinking too much, I took out a mine cart and placed onto the tracks.

"What are you doing?"

"Investigating," I told him. "Come on! It will be fun."

"I don't know," said Jerry. "We're pretty far from home base as it is. Who knows how deep that tunnel actually goes? And what if it leads us into some sort of danger?'

"We've got a whole lot of provisions of food and we've got armor on. What could possibly go wrong?"

"I guess you're right, Mike. But we should proceed on foot first," said Jerry. "What if the tracks lead down a giant hole or a pit of lava?"

But I was already inside the mine cart. All it took was one wrong move and the cart already started making its way down the tracks. At first the mine cart didn't go that fast but soon enough the tunnel started going down pretty abruptly, and so did the tracks. The mine cart started building up speed, racing through the darkness that filled the whole tunnel. I could hear Jerry behind me.

"I told you that we would proceed on foot! On foot! You've done it again, Mike!"

Apparently he got into a mine cart and started following me down the tunnel.

Within seconds, I had built up a rather great amount of speed. The tunnel began to have torches set from time to time, making it easier for me to see what was around me. I quickly saw that at certain points throughout the course of the rail line, there was a different type of rail – one that had gold parts in it. These parts of rail had a small torch next to them with a strange red orb at the top of it. The rails seemed to glow in the dark and whenever the mine cart would run over them, it seemed to give it a hefty boost in speed.

When the tunnel ended, I found myself traveling on a narrow, one block bridge above a giant lake of lava, dozens of feet below, inside a giant cave. The cave was in fact so gigantic, that I couldn't even see the ceiling.

The bridge on which I was traveling was so long that I now could see Jerry, who was not that far away from me as I thought. Apparently, once he saw me going down in my mine cart, it didn't take him that much in order to jump in his own mine cart and go down after me.

I finished crossing the bridge and found that the road went spiraling down into a deep chasm, a giant sinkhole deep into the ground. The way down was pretty steep, and the railroad was peppered with a lot of those "special rails" that boosted the speed of the mine cart as it passed over them. I was now rushing at an incredible pace. The patterns in the cave wall seemed to melt away and blend into each other. We could have passed a giant reserve of gold and iron or whatnot and I couldn't have told it.

The road abruptly went horizontally and for a moment I was afraid that I would pop out of the mine cart. Luckily, I didn't. I stayed glued to the inside of the mine cart. We then passed through yet another tunnel. The air inside the tunnel was pitch black, except for the end of it, where I could see a dim red light. We sped through the tunnel at an amazing pace and when we reached the end of it, I could see a giant cave ahead of us. The wall that was directly in front of me was half blown away revealing a beautiful forest. For a moment I was locked in time. *Where are we? Is that the…*

But I didn't have quite enough time to finish thinking about it, because the railroad came to an abrupt stop.

I fell…

Mine cart and all, I fell. The fall was pretty long, or maybe it just seemed that way, because I was taken by surprise by the abrupt stop after such a long journey.

When I finally came to my senses, I was neck-deep in water, struggling against the current to try and get to shore. By the time I got to dry land I saw that Jerry wasn't far behind me.

Jerry got out of the water and slowly walked up to me, looking in every direction, trying to get a better look at our new surroundings.

"Well, I have to say, Mike, you really outdid yourself this time. Where are we?"

"I don't know. At least it was exciting," I said to him.

"It really was. I'll give you that. But really, where in Herobrine's name are we? I mean, we…that track was really long and all of this doesn't just appear. Somebody must have built it, either a lot of people, or just some guy who had a lot of spare time and spare materials. But man, why is the last part missing?"

"I have no idea, Jerry."

"Either way, we should get a move on. If someone's out there it's better that we find him or them first."

"Should we go back, though?"

Jerry turned around and looked at me.

"Well, you were the one who was craving for adventure, weren't you?"

If my avatar could smile, it would have had the biggest grin ever on his pixelated face.

"Let's go!" I shouted.

And so we walked along the shore of the lake until we reached the exit to the forest.

It didn't take much time until we found a herd of cows, gnawing away at some patch of grass.

I quickly ran up to them and started harvesting leather and meat. From the looks of it, it was going to be quite a long adventure ahead of us, so every bit of resource counted.

Once I attacked the first cow, the others scattered into the woods. I started giving chase and Jerry wasn't far behind me. Once we managed to catch up to the last cow we saw a small wooden sign. Somehow it appeared that we had found our way to a small dirt road. The sign said: "The Village is near". The two of us followed the dirt road and in a couple of minutes we found yet another sign that said: "The Village is near," but this time the sign had another small sign behind it. That one said: "Intruders beware."

We continued our trek through the forest, following the narrow dirt road that gradually turned into a much wider gravel road. The way we saw it was that we weren't intruders. We were just travelers, explorers, adventurers on some epic quest to find some hidden civilization. After all, Minecraft is also about using your imagination, isn't it?

So we continued our travel and eventually we saw tall wooden walls and an even taller tower, also made out of wood.

"Wow, that's quite an impressive watchtower," I said to Jerry.

"It certainly is. We'd better be careful," cautioned Jerry.

When we got closer to the walls we could see that they also had quite a large wooden gate that was made out of a different type of wood than the rest of the wall. The gate was shut, though.

We got closer and closer and when we were about ten feet from the gate we heard a voice coming from the tall watchtower.

"Who are you? Stay right where you are, not a foot closer, or else," said the voice.

"We are not thieves! We're friendly," said Jerry.

"We're just travelers passing by! We came through the mountain. We found your underground railroad," I said to the voice.

There was a tense pause, after which the voice shouted.

"You what? You came through our mine? Did you steal anything? Did you destroy anything? You better not have stolen anything!"

"We didn't steal anything. We just found your railroad and it took us into that cave underneath the mountain. Honest," said Jerry.

"I'm going to let you in. But you better not do anything funny, I'm warning you. There are more of us than you, so we could easily send you to your respawn point," said the voice.

"We won't try anything funny and we won't steal anything. Promise," said Jerry.

"Okay. I'll take your word for it. I'm going to open the gate. Walk slowly. No funny business!"

And after a few seconds, the large doors opened with a "whoosh". We slowly walked past the gates and into what we discovered was the outer circle of the camp.

"That's far enough," said a guy in iron armor. He had an iron breastplate, iron grieves and iron boots but his helmet was made out of black leather. He wielded an iron sword that glowed purple.

"Stay right there", he said. "You don't look like thieves to me."

"How exactly do thieves look?" I asked him.

"Don't get smart with me, noob," he said.

"Sorry," I replied.

"So, you got this far. But in order to actually have access inside the village, you need to pay a fee."

"What fee? What are you talking about?" I asked.

"Okay we'll pay," said Jerry.

"Excellent. If you don't pay that wooden floor that you're standing on will open and you'd be swimming in quite a bit of lava. So, you just made a wise decision, my friend."

"What's the fee?" I asked.

"Well you just put some things in that wooden chest over there and one of my friends will see if it's good enough or not."

It was then that I saw that the guy wasn't alone. There were four more guys, all armed with bows, standing behind stone barricades on both our sides.

Jerry was the first one to go. He slowly walked up to the chest and deposited some goods. After he was done, it was my turn. I slowly walked up to the wooden chest and opened it. I had a lot of coal, iron and gold in my inventory. I also had quite a large amount of food and other miscellaneous blocks, such as stone, gravel and wood, but I doubted they would have been interested in that. What I also had was an emerald. But I wasn't going to give them that, now was I? After all, they couldn't search me, or anything. And so I deposited about ten blocks of gold and ten blocks of iron, as I saw that Jerry had done the same thing.

After I deposited the so-called "fee", I slowly backed away. As I backed away, an archer stepped out from behind the barricade and walked up to the chest to check the contents. He took a quick look and turned to the guy with the sword and the black helmet.

"Yup. It's okay, they can pass," said the archer.

"Did you hear that, guys? You can pass. Follow me."

The guy with the sword and the black helmet turned around and walked up to the stone wall that separated the outer area from the actual village.

The stone wall didn't have a gate like the wooden one; it had a small passage, also made from stone that had a set of iron doors on each end. When we got close enough to the passage, we saw that the iron doors were open.

We passed through the passage, walking right behind Mister Black Helmet. The four archers walked closely behind us and when the last of them passed through the passage, the set of iron doors closed behind him.

The inner yard was awesome. It seemed that behind all those walls lied a small village with houses made out of stone, bricks and wood. There was grass everywhere, and narrow gravel blocks formed intertwining roads that crawled all around and in between houses and other buildings. In the middle of the yard there were small houses, all bunched up together. They were mostly built out of wood, with a sturdy stone foundation. They had three or four small windows and a wooden door. Long-nosed villagers hustled and bustled in and out of these small houses, humming and sighing as they went about their business. Funny mobs, these villagers, they don't do much, but at least you can trade with them.

On the outer part of the yard there were a bunch of bigger houses. These ones had two or three stories and lots of windows. Some of them even had balconies, with small pots of flowers and vines on the sides of the railing. I figured that those ones belonged to the players that lived in the camp. The far most corner of the yard had a stronghold made out of grey stone bricks and some sort of dark red bricks, like nothing I had ever seen before. Finally, the yard also housed a couple of farms that had crops of wheat, carrots, pumpkins, watermelon and even some sugar cane. The farms also had some animal enclosures with some cows, chicken and a couple of sheep and a couple of pigs. What they also had, were dogs, tied up to some wooden fences. What they didn't have, were horses. I found that pretty odd, but I forgot about that detail pretty soon when I saw something else that drew my attention.

We finally reached the stronghold, after walking across the entire village, as the stronghold was directly opposite to the gates and the stone passage.

The stronghold opened its gate and out came a guy that was wearing a full set of diamond armor and who wielded a diamond sword. The guy slowly walked up to us.

"Greetings, guys! My name's Micah, I'm the leader of this clan and sort of the…mayor, if you will."

"Hi. I'm Jerry and this is my friend, Mike."

"Nice to meet you. How did you guys get here?"

"Well, we found this…" I never got to finish my sentence because Jerry quickly intervened.

"We found this railway and decided to, you know, take a ride and see where it gets us. We're sort of traveling around. We're adventurers."

What Jerry said, or rather what he didn't say made me very curious. I made a mental note to ask him about it when we had a chance to talk in private.

Micah didn't seem to pay any attention to the situation.

"Awesome. We don't get many visitors these days. This place was really popular some time ago, a lot of players coming and going, building and crafting all sorts of stuff. But, some griefers spawned one day, a whole bunch of them. They really ruined it for everybody. Players started leaving, few remained. Eventually, the griefers left. But they left some things behind. Some bad, some good."

"They left bad things behind?" I asked Micah.

"Yeah. I don't really want to focus on that," said Micah.

"Fair enough. So what happened when they left?" Jerry asked him.

"Well, a few of us remained, me and Zeke over there," said Micah, pointing at Mr. Black Helmet. "We found this village and rebuilt it. Then these four guys came along with Trent, the guy from the tower. They were a clan in search of a place of their own. We became friends and formed a new clan and rebuilt the village as you see it now."

"Impressive," said Jerry.

"It really is, isn't it? And you haven't seen even half of it," said Micah, probably bursting of pride. "You can stay with us for tonight, but if you decide to join us and our clan, you are welcome to stay for however long you want."

"How can we join your clan?" I asked Micah.

"Eh, we will have all the time in the world to talk about that tomorrow. You guys just take a tour of the place. You'll find that our Inn has good accommodations, even if we haven't had any guests in it for quite a while. I'll talk to you tomorrow."

And with that, Micah went back inside his stronghold, followed by all of the archers, who by then had placed their bows within their inventories. The only one who remained in the yard with us was Zeke, who had to be our tour guide for the day.

"So. Sorry about the 'warm' reception, guys. We don't get many players around here, just like the boss said," said Zeke, our new "friend". "Micah really got upset when those griefers came around. We really don't take kind to strangers poking their pickaxes in our business."

Jerry and I looked at each other.

"We're not griefers, you know," said Jerry.

"Right, right, I believe you. I do, really."

He took us around the village showed us the farms and how they work. Apparently they had some sort of contraptions built so that the eggs from the chicken would get collected instantly inside a chest. They also had all sorts of weird contraptions that automated their crops. I had never seen things like those before, which wasn't all that surprising, considering how big of a noob I was, but the most interesting part was that not even Jerry had seen most of those contraptions. When Jerry asked about a particular contraption that had some sort of red circuitry running through it, Zeke just brushed off the question saying that Micah was "the brains" behind that particular one and that only he knew how to build them. Zeke also specified that there was another location that had a huge wheat and vegetable farm, but it's off-limits to strangers, or rather "new acquaintances," as he put it.

The second part of our tour was about the houses, the player houses that is, which by the way, did not have any form of security on them. The doors were made out of iron and you could open them with a simple press of a button.

We stepped inside Zeke's house, which was the only one that we were allowed to see the inside.

"It's not much, but I like it!" said Zeke.

The interior was pretty nice looking. The floor was made out of dark wood, the windows were pretty big and let in a lot of light. Torches hung from the wooden beams that went across some of the walls. To be honest, Zeke had a lot of nice objects inside his house. He had a jukebox, carpets, potted plants, armor racks and all sorts of stuff. Upstairs he had a nice bedroom with a whole lot of paintings, a crafting table and a furnace. What caught my eye, though, was a funny looking lamp that he had on the side of his bed. It was made out of a weird looking block that radiated a warm light.

I couldn't help but ask.

"Hey, Zeke! What is that?"

"It's a lamp, man, obviously," he laughed.

"But where did you get the materials?"

"I got that glow stone from the Nether. Where else?"

"The Nether?"

"Precisely. We make regular trips to the Nether. You find all sorts of stuff there. But it's pretty dangerous, though. One false move and you're either toast or you get completely lost. It's really simple to do both of them. Compasses don't work in the Nether and neither do maps, by the way. So unless you stick together with your guys or pay close attention to what you're doing and where you're going…"

"You get lost and you die, I get it…"I said. "It's pretty dangerous right here, too."

"Oh yes. Make no mistake: The Overworld is pretty dangerous, too. But there are things in The Nether that can scare the spots of a cow, if you know what I mean." said Zeke

I didn't know what he meant, but I sort of got the bigger picture.

When we finished seeing the upper part of his house, we went down the stairs and I saw a lever and an opening in the wall next to it.

"Hey, Zeke! What's that?"

"What's what? You mean that? It's the basement. You're not allowed in there. It's off limits for strangers."

I looked at Jerry and remained silent. I bet that he found that odd as much as I did.

Anyway, Zeke then escorted us to the Inn, as the day was almost over. The Inn was essentially a small house, one of those that were huddled up together in the middle of the yard. This particular house had only one room in it. The room had a crafting table and a furnace; a chest that had some loaves of bread and some apples in it and four beds. I wondered why there were only four beds in there. I mean, did they never have more than four players as guests in their camp?

But, as I walked up to one of the beds, it dawned on me! These weren't real beds; they were made out of wood and carpets. Of course! They wouldn't want strangers to sleep in their village. That way the strangers would keep respawning there.

That being said, we couldn't sleep that night and we couldn't go out and about, roaming the village – Zeke was kind of clear on that one that unless we joined the clan. As guests we were not allowed to roam the premises at night. And so we were basically prisoners, for the time being. Time usually flies when you're doing interesting stuff in Minecraft, not when you're sitting around in a small shack and waiting for the day to come. At least the two of us had some time to talk privately about all the weird stuff that we saw that day.

I went first.

"These guys seem pretty strange to me."

"They don't just seem pretty strange, they really are strange. I don't know what it is, but they just put out this bad vibe about them," said Jerry.

"Oh, I've been meaning to ask you this: why did you interrupt me when I was about to say that we were in that abandoned mineshaft?"

"I didn't want them to know about it. I didn't think that it would have been wise. I mean, you saw the way that they treated us. Their tunnel led straight through to the abandoned mineshaft, the abandoned mineshaft from which we gathered almost all of the visible resources. What if they thought that it's their mineshaft and their resources and that we stole all of their stuff? I mean that railroad was obviously built by them. Although I don't really know why the end was missing."

I guess Jerry was right. I certainly didn't trust these guys. There was something strange about them.

The next morning, just when the sun went up, we received visitors. Micah and Zeke entered the Inn.

"Rise and shine, my friends. I hope you enjoyed your stay at our Inn and I hope that you understand the reason behind the nature of accommodations," said Micah.

"You mean the reason why you didn't give us any beds", I said to him.

"Exactly! We don't really want strangers setting spawning points in our village, now do we?"

"It's perfectly understandable," said Jerry.

"So? Have you guys decided yet? Are you going to join our village and our clan?"

Jerry and I had talked about this before these guys had come. We already had everything planned out.

"I'll join your clan, Micah," said Jerry.

"I won't," I said.

Micah was silent for a moment. After that he said:

"Cool. We have got a new member. That's nice. Welcome to the clan, Jerry. I hope you'll like living in our village and mining and crafting with us."

He then turned to me:

"Well, I hope you enjoyed your stay. But considering your negative answer in joining our clan, you need to leave right now. Thanks. Zeke here will escort you out of the village. My advice is to avoid coming back here. Have a nice day."

Well he didn't seem to take that well. At least he didn't kill. At least not right away.

The four of us walked out of the Inn. Micah and Jerry went to the stronghold and Zeke and I slowly walked toward the gate. The rain poured down furiously. My bodyguard and I walked through the stone passage. When we reached the outer yard I saw that the archers were there again and had their arrows pointed at me. I was feeling a bit uneasy, but I figured that they wouldn't keep Jerry as a member and then two minutes later would kill me…and I was right. The archers kept their arrows and let me walk out of there. As I walked out of the encampment, the huge wooden gates closed behind me.

It was now time for part two of our plan: I had to get to a safe distance and keep an eye out for any suspicious activity from the guys in the village. Jerry would do basically the same thing except he would spy on them from within, which was more dangerous. I had to count seven days from that day and then meet Jerry at our secret place in order for us to see what the other had found out.

But now, I had to use everything that Jerry had taught me about Minecraft in order to survive.

My inventory was quite full. Jerry and I decided what the best items and resources that we both had were, and I took them all in order to maximize my chances of survival out here in the wild.

I never stopped wondering about what Jerry was doing, from the moment I set my first step outside that village.

I started running like crazy through the forest, but I only ran in one single direction. I couldn't leave a trail behind because I could not risk to be found by the guys from the village.

I ran for the whole day, until I came out of the forest and found myself on top of a small hill. From the small hill I saw a small house in the distance. I kept running until I got close enough to see the light from within the house. The sun had set completely and darkness had fallen over the land. I peered from behind a tall oak to see if I could spot any movement. I saw two people placing torches around some wheat crops. A small fence made out of wood surrounded the house. These guys even had a dog that was tied up to a fence post next to the house. They wore leather armor, so I guessed that they hadn't been in Minecraft for that long a period of time. Their swords were made out of iron, though. I got a chance to see the swords because the moment they spotted me they took them out and started running towards me.

"Hey! You there!"

"Wait! I'm friendly!" I shouted.

"Are you from the village?"

###

Made in the USA
Charleston, SC
28 January 2015